T0146906

MAGDALENA

MAGDALENA

A COLONIAL GIRL'S EPIC JOURNEY

Cara Dunkelberger

MAGDALENA
A COLONIAL GIRL'S EPIC JOURNEY

This is a work of fiction. All of the characters, names, incidents, organizations, and dialogue in this novel are either the products of the author's imagination or are used fictitiously.

iUniverse books may be ordered through booksellers or by contacting:

iUniverse
1663 Liberty Drive
Bloomington, IN 47403
www.iuniverse.com
1-800-Authors (1-800-288-4677)

Because of the dynamic nature of the Internet, any web addresses or links contained in this book may have changed since publication and may no longer be valid. The views expressed in this work are solely those of the author and do not necessarily reflect the views of the publisher, and the publisher hereby disclaims any responsibility for them.

Any people depicted in stock imagery provided by Thinkstock are models, and such images are being used for illustrative purposes only.
Certain stock imagery © Thinkstock.

ISBN: 978-1-5320-2592-1 (sc)
ISBN: 978-1-5320-2593-8 (e)

Library of Congress Control Number: 2017909490

Print information available on the last page.

iUniverse rev. date: 07/18/2017

PREFACE

While visiting Berks County PA, I happened upon an intriguing story of a group of Germanic immigrants who left Europe for America in 1709. I had assumed that Germanics of that time came to Berks by way of Philadelphia. These did not, but rather via upstate New York.

This fictional novelette is based on well-documented hardships that history thrust upon the thousands who in 1709 left the Palatine area of the Rhine, then part of the Holy Roman Empire. It is written from the perspective of my seventh great-grandmother Elizabetha Magdalena Loesch, a child among them.

The Palatine Families of New York by Henry Z Jones, Jr., was an invaluable source of information.

MAGDALENA'S DIARY

A Berks County PA newspaper clipping from 1870 recorded that a very old diary had been found in the attic of a farmhouse. It had been written in a kind of German similar to Pennsylvania Dutch and told the story of a little girl, Magdalena, who was content on her family farm near the Rhine River in 1708. But within a year her life drastically changed.

There was a note tucked in the diary, perhaps written by one of Magdalena's descendants, that said Magdalena had been almost eight years old when she began her diary. It also said Adam, her oldest brother, was four years older than she and her brother George, one year older.

In 1708 Magdalena also had had an infant brother Jacob. Her only sister, Susannah, named for her mother, had died as a baby. Her maternal grandmother *Grossmami*, widow of a shepherd, lived with them.

My baptismal name is Elizabetha Magdalena. *Mami* calls me that when I'm naughty. She says, "Elizabetha Magadalena, come in here and make your bed!"

Our *Dawdi* and my brothers mostly call me "Molly."

We live on a farm where my big brother Adam helps Dawdi care for our animals, hunt deer and rabbits, and till the soil. We grow flax, wheat, rye, oats, grapes, and other things. Dawdi makes wine from our grapes and sells it at the market near the Rhine River. He makes beer, too, that he and Adam drink.

Adam and I are skinny and have blonde hair and blue eyes like Mami. My brother George is only a year older than I am, and he's fatter. His hair and eyes are brown like my baby brother Jacob's and Dawdi's.

I can't read or write because girls don't go to school. So, I asked Adam if he would please write my stories in a diary when he's not too busy working, like some rainy evenings.

"Yes, Molly," he said. "I'll do that for you."

Yesterday started good, but became sad. After breakfast Mami and I cleared off our big wooden table. We washed the dishes with water we brought from the spring.

She reminded me, "*Raus!* Go out! Feed the chickens. George, go with her."

I have my own special jobs. I keep the chickens happy and collect and clean eggs. Sometimes I feed our horse and cows. I help pick beans and peas. Mami and Adam gather the other vegetables like cabbage, turnips, and brussels sprouts. In the fall we all have fun bringing in pumpkins.

After I filled a small sack with the barley that Dawdi had crushed with a hammer, I ran to the chicken pen. I hummed the Lutheran hymn that I know how to play on the little zither Dawdi had made for me. The sun was bright, and the warm air felt good. It made leaves dance in the apple trees.

George ran toward me with his sack of feed and threw some at me.

"George! Stop that! I'll get Adam after you!"

I scolded him and threw feed back at him.

"Come here, Cluck-Cluck," I called to my favorite hen. She has a cute little chick named Peeps. I like to pet Peeps. She follows me around.

"What's that?" George asked, pointing at the sky.

I thought he might be looking at smoke from fires set by French soldiers. Mami says they're Catholic and started destroying our lands before I was born. Now they march through here and cross the Rhine to fight other people. They steal our food and trample our fields. Sometimes they even sleep in our house. Mami sleeps with me when that happens because I'm scared of them.

I looked for smoke in the sky over the forest. We never go there because it's full of witches who eat little children. But I didn't see any smoke.

"Where?" I asked. "I don't see anything."

"Yes, I do! Look! Look!" George pointed over the stone chimney of our log home.

"Oh, there... just a big bird."

All of a sudden it swooped down close to us. It had a very big hooked beak. I didn't want its feet to get tangled in my long hair. We started running away. The chickens were making lots of noise and running over each other. The bird grabbed poor Cluck-Cluck. Our Schnauzer Willie barked loudly and chased the bird away.

"No, no!" I screamed as I ran to save my poor hen. But she didn't move. I burst into tears. The air became still, and the leaves stopped dancing. I tripped and fell as I ran for help.

"Mami! Mami! A bird hurt Cluck-Cluck! Bad!"

George was running around with a stick helping our dog to keep the bird from coming back.

"Oh, dear!" Mami put her arms around me and said, "Look, Peeps is fine."

She pointed to Peeps and asked, "Should we get a big bowl of water and let Peeps swim around in it?"

I nodded yes and dried my tears with my apron.

She said after I wash up, we would bury Cluck-Cluck. My skirt was muddy from my fall.

When Dawdi and Adam came back from the fields at noon for dinner they dug a grave. We said a prayer and sang a hymn, "A...bide with me," like we did when we buried my baby sister. I felt very sad. I picked some wildflowers and put them on her grave.

"*Kum esse!*" Mami called us all to eat.

Her warm fresh bread smelled good. She made barley porridge with vegetables and my favorite, wheat dumplings and sauerkraut. We set the table with dishes decorated with birds and flowers. The distelfink bird was my favorite.

Dawdi sat at the head of the table. We thanked God for our food and I asked Jesus to take care of Cluck-Cluck.

A tear fell into my porridge. I couldn't eat. My stomach was too upset.

The snow is still very deep. I'm cold and hungry. Our trees are dead. Animals and birds froze to death. Our neighbor Hans told Dawdi he's never known a winter so cold in all his ninety years. Grossmami died in January because she was too cold and hungry.

Last night I was supposed to be asleep in my loft bed near the chimney, away from our damp, cold earthen floor. But I didn't go to sleep right away. I wanted to listen to Mami and Dawdi downstairs in their *kammer*, sleeping area.

"Dearest Susannah, we *have* to go. We'll starve here! We have to sell our land. And sell the only cow and horse we still have."

Mami was crying softly.

Dawdi continued, "Our plows, tools, and spinning wheel will fetch some money, too. Then we can pay the prince's departure tax and get a boat to Rotterdam."

"I can't understand why he makes us pay to leave! He gets tax money from us all the time."

"He's greedy."

"God will punish him."

"We should listen to the men at the river market. They talk about free land in America. They say Queen Anne will help us."

"But places like Carolina, Pennsylvania, and New York are so far away!"

"Herr Braun is going soon. So is the Zeh family."

"I don't understand why they think the queen will help."

"There are too many French Catholics in America. She needs Protestants like us."

After a pause, he added, "We'll work on her land to pay for our ocean passage, then get our own farmland."

"Are you sure this is true?"

"Yes, I saw the *Golden Book*. You know, the little book Pastor Kocherthal wrote a few years ago. Somebody was reading it out loud at the river marketplace. Kocherthal's group of families is already in America."

I'm proud that Dawdi can read and is so wise.

"What if it's not the truth?" Mami still didn't believe the rumors, but I did.

Dawdi answered her. "I think it's true. Forty more farmers left last year. They got passage and free American land and tools to work it. Remember William Penn, the Englishman? He helped the Quakers go to Pennsylvania a long time ago. There are pamphlets about that."

"I pray you're right, Baltzer. I will obey you. You know best."

Mami started up the ladder. She thought I was sleeping and quietly kissed my cheek. I dreamed about a warm sunny farm in America.

After the river ice melted we packed some of our belongings and got on a boat to Rotterdam. Dawdi sold our spinning wheel and most everything else.

I carried our drop spindle in my bundle so we can spin flax at our new home. The little iron spinning rod that goes through it makes it heavy, but I'll be strong and carry it anyway.

A rooster crowing woke me. I didn't know where I was. It wasn't my familiar bed.

Then I heard Philip, the oldest Braun boy, talking to his brothers and remembered that his family had traveled with us on the same boat to Rotterdam.

We'd been on the Rhine for *five* weeks. Sometimes there was no wind. Sometimes the wind was too strong. When the weather was bad they made us get off the boat to wait.

Now we're waiting to cross to England. English boats were supposed to take us to London, but they didn't come. Last night I heard little froggies chirping, so I know it's springtime. My shadow is getting shorter, too.

The people who live here talk a strange language. Dawdi said they call us Palatines. There are more than ten thousand of us.

We all sleep in shacks or outdoors. Our whole family sleeps in one small shack with a roof made of reeds.

"You awake, Molly?" Mami asked. "Pour water on some oats for breakfast then come to the river with me and baby Jacob to wash."

I took a clay bowl to fill with river water and went with Mami to the ladies' area. I checked for any boys peeping through the woods. Some did that to see us naked. I saw no one. It was safe to undress.

"Mami, I'm finished. May I go play with the ducklings way down there, past the bathing areas?" I pointed.

"Yes, but not for long," she called over her shoulder as she headed to the ration lines.

As I walked behind the boundary of the men's bathing area, I heard Philip Braun. I couldn't see him, but I recognized his voice and the voice of Martin, one of his brothers. Then I noticed the figure of a small boy in his underwear crouching near the water.

"Shhh…get his britches and give 'em to me," Philip told Martin.

I realized the little boy was Hans, their youngest brother.

I moved to get a better look. When Philip got Hans' britches, he threw them up over a tree branch. Then he sneaked up behind Hans and pushed him into the cold water!

Hans gasped and stood in waist-deep water.

"Help! I'm freezing!"

His brothers laughed and shouted, *"Schnell geiste! Schnell geiste!"*

They blamed a mischievous spirit. As they ran away, I giggled softly.

I turned my back when Hans began to scramble ashore. I doubted he'd find his britches and didn't know what to do. He must have been very cold! I was thankful that one of the Zeh boys saw the whole thing and shouted at Hans to look in the nearby tree.

Later we all gathered in the area where the ducks lived and laughed about Hans. My brother George came to see what we were laughing at.

"Let's play tag!" he suggested to everybody. For a little while I was happy again.

Three months ago some important Englishmen came to our shacks in Rotterdam. Herr Braun said they were sending families across the water to their country. They spoke a kind of German different than ours, but we could understand.

"Are you Catholic?" one of the them asked a family near us.

The father nodded.

"Get your family and come with me. You have to go back home."

Then he pointed to Dawdi.

"You Catholic?"

"Lutheran."

"How many?"

Dawdi waved his hand to tell us to stand close to him.

The man was writing a list and asked, "Name? How old? Farmer?"

"Baltzer Lesch, 38, farmer and vinedresser."

Then Dawdi pointed to each of us.

"Wife, son 14, daughter 9, son 8, son 2."

"Go to the dock at dawn to cross to London. Understand?"

Dawdi nodded.

"Next."

"John Zeh 42, wife, sons, 1, 6, and infant, Catholic. Farmer and vinedresser."

The Englishman hesitated and looked at our two families.

"Together?"

"Yes."

"Be at the dock at dawn," he said to Herr Zeh.

We were glad he didn't make them go back home with other Catholics. Mami hugged Frau Zeh and they both smiled.

The next day we got on a boat and spent six days sailing across the water to Plymouth, near London. I didn't mind being on the boat. I was tired of living in a noisy shack and eating bad food.

Now it's October and we're still in London. We're all very unhappy and tired of waiting. Some people say the *Golden Book* wasn't true.

Our tent is in a big field full of tall grass. There are hundreds of tents here. Five other big fields are full of people, too. It smells bad. Many are sick. There's no good place to wash and not much room for all of us to sleep in our tent. Little Jacob cries all the time and looks sickly.

At first, the English were kind. They called us "poor Palatines" and helped feed us. Now they hate us for eating their food. Some of our men were attacked by them with axes and hammers.

Dawdi had news today.

"We're going to America! The Queen needs us to help make stuff from pine trees there. Pitch and tar for her navy."

"Where?" Mami asked.

"New York. They'll send us there to work for a while. Then we'll get our own land!"

"Farmland?"

"Yes, forty acres! Our very own!"

"And no more paying taxes to a Palatine prince!"

Adam asked Dawdi, "Are you *sure* they're not sending us someplace else? I heard some got sent to Ireland. And some to places called Carolina and Jamaica."

"Queen Anne wants us in New York. God has blessed us. It has good farmland."

A few weeks ago, word spread quickly from family to family.

"Pack your things. We're moving out!"

"*Macht schnell! Schnell!* Hurry up!"

Somebody pointed to the sky and said, "The weather's too bad to cross the ocean! Clouds are dark! *Dunkle!* Where are we going?"

"I don't know where. They said they'll be back late morning to take us somewhere."

Mami said, "Molly, take care of little Jacob while Dawdi and I pack. Adam and George, help us."

We didn't have much, only one change of clothing each, a few pots and dishes, and the drop spindle. I had to leave my zither and dolly behind in Rotterdam. Dawdi said he'll build a new zither for me in America.

"Follow me. Stay close," one Englishman yelled.

"You, you, and you!" He pointed to us, the Brauns, and the Zehs. "Captain Wilken's ship. The *Providens.*"

I was happy we'd be with families we knew. There were nine other ships.

"Sail? When?" Dawdi tried to ask with hand motions and words. None of us speak English.

"Better weather," he said, but we didn't understand.

Herr Weiser heard and translated. "We'll live aboard ship until good weather, and no French warships, and no pirates. Spring."

"Spring! That's many months from now!"

He said the local people don't like us living in the fields. So they were moving us to ships. That sounded like fun. I'd never been on a big ship.

Philip Braun noticed I was having trouble with Jacob. He was weak and couldn't walk well.

Philip asked, "May I help you carry him?"

"*Ya, danke,*" I said and blushed.

I think Philip's handsome. Dawdi met his father selling wine at the river a few years ago and says Philip is a nice boy. He has six brothers and sisters.

Dawdi knows Herr Zeh, too. His children are very young and Frau Zeh is expecting another one. They asked my brother Adam to be baptismal sponsor if it's a boy.

Our family went onboard and found space below deck to pile our things. We tied everything with rope because the ship was rocking back and forth. I had trouble walking.

On that first day I asked, "Jacob has to pee-pee. Where should I take him, Mami?"

She asked Dawdi, "Up there?" She pointed to a line at a little door at the front of the boat.

He nodded. "Or those buckets, there. Then dump it into the sea."

The first night I couldn't fall asleep. So, I imagined America and our own farm. But a rat ran across my legs.

May 1710, At Sea

We've been at sea many weeks. I hate it. Somebody's little boy got so sick that he died. They had to throw him overboard. We said prayers and sang hymns, but it seemed so cruel. He's with Jesus now.

Each of us has a hammock to sleep in. At first, I was excited to try mine. But it often feels wet and smells strange, like dirt after a rainstorm. The boat rocks, children cry, and people snore.

Our food is terrible, salt pork and beef and ships biscuits. They call it hard tack. It has weevils in it. Sometimes there's cheese or beans or lard for the biscuits. There's never very much. Last week some people tried to steal our food. We should have stayed home even if it was so cold!

No one is healthy. Some got rashes and fevers from lice bites. Dawdi got a little rash yesterday.

Mami and I slept on the top deck last night. It's better up there but it's hard to find space. The sky was full of dark clouds and the boat rocked hard, one side to the other. I was afraid I'd fall off. I couldn't stand up and had to vomit.

"Here," Adam said. He'd noticed my problem and handed me a bucket. He's such a good big brother and I love him very much.

Then the wind got stronger and it began to pour. We held onto the railing and made our way below deck.

Adam tried to cheer us. "I borrowed Edward's whistle. Want to hear music called a hornpipe?"

A young shipmate, Edward, who spoke some German had become Adam's friend. He'd taught Adam to play his whistle.

I felt a little happier when I listened to the lively tune.

Philip Braun and my brother George came to listen, too.

"Won't it be good when we can dance to music on our own farm in America?" Philip dreamed.

"And eat sauerkraut and dumplings," George mused.

"And *hinkelwelschkann-nudle supp*!" said Philip. "I love chicken, corn, noodle soup!"

"I want to breathe fresh air!" I added.

George assured me, "Each family will have forty acres of its very own! No princes who collect tax!"

"Want to tell stories?" I suggested fairy tales Grandma had taught me.

"No, how about dice?" Adam asked and didn't wait for an answer. "I'll get some from Edward. He's working now and isn't using them."

The rocking got worse. The dice rolled around too much. We staggered back to our families' little areas. A cask came loose and hit me. I fell and got up on my hands and knees to crawl. My knees were scraped open, so I dabbed them with my apron. What a shame to ruin the pretty apron I embroidered long ago. Then I gave up and just let them bleed. They were hidden under my skirt.

An hour later, after the storm went away, Mami needed me.

"Help me mend some things. Get George's britches."

I took his dirty extra pair and started stitching a tear in the linen.

"Is there a pan of ocean water to wash them, Mami?"

"No, it spilled during the storm."

She continued, "Dawdi just told me he has a bad headache. The rash on his back is spreading. Baby Jacob has a fever and is very weak."

That made me very worried about Dawdi and Jacob. I'm scared they might die. So I say extra prayers throughout each day.

One day last June, George jumped up and down on the boat deck.

"Look! Look! Land!" Seagulls were flying over a big dark area in the water.

We'd been at sea so long that I thought we were lost. Everyone was very happy to see land.

But when we docked in New York they made us stay on our boat because people who lived there didn't want us near them. They thought our sick people would make them sick. Days later some Englishmen got tents for us to put up on an island.

As we prepared to get off the boat, Edward came to say goodbye. He told Adam there were nine other ships full of Palatine people like us. In total, five hundred people had died at sea. More than two thousand were still alive.

He also said there was a ship on the ocean going to England from America with four Indian chiefs on it. They were going to visit Queen Anne. Edward once saw drawings of Indians who wore feathers. I knew strange people lived in America, but I had never seen a picture of them.

When we finally left the ship to go to tents on an island, Englishmen made Dawdi go to a special area for sick people. They said there weren't enough doctors to cut them and take out their bad blood.

Thank the Lord that Jacob is feeling better and lives in our tent.

But a few weeks after we got off the ship, a bad Englishman came and took George away! He was so brave *he* didn't cry, but Mami and I did.

"*Du moosht. Du moosht.*" Mami told George he *must* go, as tears ran down her cheeks.

I wanted to kick the man on his shin, but Mami wouldn't let me. She said they had to take away all the boys between eight and twelve years old.

Then she explained, "Governor Hunter of New York is making George live with a man who will teach him to weave. He will help the man, and that man will feed him. Hunter doesn't have enough money to feed all of us."

Now it's fall. I know that because the trees are turning pretty colors like they did back home. We no longer live in tents on the island.

Mami, Adam, Jacob, I, and many others were put on boats and sent a long way up the Hudson River. Dawdi is still in the sick area near the harbor. We're too far away to ever see him. And George is with the weaver, too far away for us to see him. We worry about them and say prayers. Mami cries a lot. We don't even know if they're still alive.

The English said Queen Anne bought this forest land for us. When we got here, they shouted orders: "You men come with me. Take an ax and pick. We're going to clear land for your village."

Adam goes with them every day to clear this thick forest land and make crude log huts. Right now there aren't enough huts, so we have to share them.

Neighbors told us what they learned from the English.

"There are going to be seven villages cleared by us. Some on this side of the Hudson River and some on the other side."

Another neighbor said, "That will take a long time! Will there be enough food? I don't understand why we don't have the farmland they promised!"

"They say they'll give us food. Every village has to choose one man who can read and write. A *listmaster*, they'll call him. He'll write how many adults and children there are in each family. Big families will get more rations."

It's true that food is given, but it's never enough and tastes bad... dried meat, fish, cheese, flour, peas. I long for some fresh food like we had on our farm.

They say we won't get our own land until we pay our way here. We have to make stuff from the pine trees for the queen's navy. They also say every family will be given warm clothes, cloth, soap, one cow per family, a horse, pigs, farm tools, and guns.

We're living in our forest village. Before the snows came, we built our own small log hut. Herr Kopf helped us after he built his own hut for himself and his daughter Sophia. The rest of his family died in the sick camp. The Braun and Zeh families helped us, too. We've been near them ever since we went down the Rhine two years ago.

To build our hut, the men dug into the ground in the shape of a rectangle. Then they made walls by stacking logs up each side. The logs are held together with clay. They made a roof with more logs and clay, then covered it with bark. It mostly keeps out the rain and snow.

In January a group of men built a schoolhouse that looks like our huts. Boys go there part of each day except Sunday to learn reading, writing, and other things. I wish I could go.

Last week Dawdi came to live with us again! I'm so happy about that! But I wish we could see George. He's been away such a long time.

Dawdi is still very weak. When a reverend visits our camp of log huts on Sundays, he prays for Dawdi. I say extra prayers for him, too, while I hold the small cross Adam made for me.

Last Sunday Mami said, "The snow's stopping. Let's walk to Herr Braun's for church."

Adam and I always go with her.

She asked Dawdi, "Baltzer, may we leave Jacob here?"

"No, please take him with you. He tries to leave our hut. I can't go after him."

So she told Adam to bring Jacob.

Adam is as tall as Dawdi now. His voice is low and he has a beard. He was a baptismal sponsor for the Zeh's baby son whom they named "Adam."

By the time we arrived at the gathering place for church, my feet were very cold. We huddled around a big fire outside for the service because there are too many of us to fit into one hut.

The pine trees smelled good. I saw deer watching us from the woods and wondered if the evil forest witches kill deer, or just little boys and girls.

"Let us pray," our German reverend began the service, and we all bowed our heads.

My mind wandered during the long prayer. I thought about Indians. Someone had told me that our reverend could speak Indian language. When he came to New York long ago, he taught Indians to speak English and helped them become Protestant. Some Indians were even baptized! They call them "praying Indians." French people in Canada taught other Indians how to become Catholic. I wondered if Indians look like birds when they wear feathers. Could they fly?

"Amen," everyone said, and I stopped daydreaming. At the end of the service, we sang Luther's "A Mighty Fortress Is Our God."

"*Ein feste burg ist unser Gott…*"

I love that hymn. It makes be feel safe and happy.

After church Adam and Jacob started walking back. I waited for Mami while she talked to some ladies.

One of the ladies said, "Herr Conrad Weiser is a good listmaster for us. He used to be a corporal in the military, you know. Very smart man."

"How old is Conrad Jr.?" Mami asked.

"About the same as your Adam."

Frau Zeh added, "There's trouble in that family. Conrad is full of hate for his step-mother…too strict."

Jesus teaches us to love, not hate, I thought. Then I imagined how very sad Conrad must have been when his mother died.

One woman said in a voice loud enough for everyone to hear, "Listmaster Weiser says when the Indian chiefs visited Queen Anne a few years ago, they told her they wanted to help us poor Palatines. They gave her land called Schoharie for us. Good farmland."

"*Sko-harry*? That's a strange name!" I thought.

"I can't understand why Governor Hunter won't let us go there," that woman continued.

Then all the women began talking at once. They didn't agree with one another about moving away without Hunter's permission.

"We're refusing to plant seeds here. I thought our protest would make Hunter let us go."

"It doesn't seem to be doing any good. Hunter still says we cannot go to Schoharie."

"We should take that land directly from the Indians! We'll never have farms where we are!"

"Yes, directly from the Indians!"

"We should go! They're not giving us enough food!"

"Provisions are bad."

"Too dangerous to leave."

"They never gave us flax to make clothes."

"Our demands don't matter."

"My Phillip thinks we should go."

"Indians might attack us. I'm afraid."

"We *do* owe Queen Anne enough work here to pay our passage. We must stay."

Just then I saw an Indian boy in the pines!

His skin was a different color than ours. His clothes were the color of deer. He had arrows in a sling over his shoulder, like the one I found in the woods last week.

"Mami! Over there!"

I pointed, but he was gone. It was the first time I saw one of them. I wasn't scared. He didn't look mean or angry.

We almost had a battle with the English last week.

"Get all our men...bring guns, meet here," Herr Braun yelled to anyone who could hear him.

"Hurry, be strong!"

"*Schnell! Schnell!*"

Hundreds came. Mami and I were at the creek and ran back to our hut.

"Baltzer, there's going to be war," she told Dawdi.

"The English have taken our listmasters and won't free them. They're angry that we refuse to plant."

Dawdi started trying to get up. "I must go!"

"No, don't leave us! You're too weak!"

We sat on his lap so he couldn't get up.

"I pray they'll talk instead of shooting!"

"Where's Adam?"

"I don't know!"

Out of breath from running, Adam burst into our hut.

"No shooting. Listmasters free. Not harmed. Saw them."

"That's a relief!"

"Now they're arguing over our contract with the English. Hunter says we didn't make enough pitch and tar for their navy. We still owe them two years' work."

"It's no better than back home. We're slaves here, just like we were slaves to the prince," Mami complained. "I want the rich farmland they promised!"

"That farmland must be at Schoharie, a hundred miles away!" Adam added. "We're trapped here!" Mami was still upset.

This week everyone agreed to start planting corn, peas, onions, carrots, beets, turnips, and cabbage. I want to help Mami tend our crops, but we girls and boys must gather things off the forest ground. The English call them pine knots and showed us what they look like. We're all scared because of the witches in the woods.

Mami tells us, "Du moosht!"

Just like she told George he *must* go to learn to weave, we *must* gather pine knots.

Adam helps the men try to make navy stuff from pines. But nobody can tell them how to do it. The English don't know how!

All of us Palatines used to be good friends, but now some families argue with others. Some want to leave for Schoharie. Others want to stay here.

Philip Braun was confirmed at our Sunday service this week. Whenever he smiles at me, I still blush. My friend Catharina Feck teases me about him.

By next year *I'll* be old enough to get confirmed, too. My chest is starting to get two bumps on it like the older girls have.

After the service I heard one lady tell another, "My Johannes said the pines here in New York are the wrong kind for making naval stuff. They're not like pines in Carolina where they make naval stuff. And he said the English now know that. But they make us try anyway."

I started wondering what was to become of us. A voice interrupted my thoughts.

"*Guten tag! Wie bischt?* How is your father, Molly?"

It was Philip!

I didn't want to start sobbing in front of him, but managed to answer.

"I'm afraid the Lord wants to take him soon. I can't bear it! The cold weather is making him worse. He says his whole body pains him and sunlight hurts his eyes."

"I'll say extra prayers for him."

"Ya, please do. Mami and I take turns staying with him. He likes when I sing hymns, especially "Now Rest Beneath Night's Shadow.""

I sang the first line. "*Nun ruhen alle Walder....*"

"But when Dawdi says, 'That's nice, my dear Molly,' I have to hold back my tears to keep singing. Sometimes he gets confused and calls me by his mother's name."

We were silent for a moment.

"Does your family need help with men's work?" Adam asked.

"*Nein, danke.* Dawdi asked Herr Kopf to help us. He has only one daughter, Adam's age. The rest of his family died. He helps Adam do our men's work."

"I thought Herr Kopf was in Canada. Didn't he go to help Governor Hunter invade there?"

"Ya, but they all came back very soon. Governor Hunter changed his plans. Herr Kopf says nobody likes Hunter. He's very greedy."

"May I walk with you to your hut?"

I nodded.

"*Danke.* I'll tell Adam he can stay to talk to Conrad."

"Where's little Jacob?"

"Home with Mami and Dawdi. I think he doesn't want to leave Dawdi."

Last winter was the worst of my life, even worse than the really cold one back on our own farm. Shortly after Christmas, Dawdi became very sick and died. He had told me to be brave and help Mami and Herr Kopf. I still cry for him, even though I know he's in Heaven with Jesus.

Sometimes I expect to see him when other men gather to talk. But he's never with them. I prayed God would let him come back for my Confirmation in March. But he didn't. I thought maybe he died because I didn't pray enough. Was it my fault? Did I do something bad?

"No, my dear Molly," Mami said. "It wasn't your fault. It was God's plan."

Dawdi had told Mami that if he died, she should marry Herr Kopf, if he asked her. Herr Kopf is a good *shteef-dawdi* and nice man, but I don't love him the same way I loved Dawdi. I get angry when he tries to do things for us that Dawdi should be doing. I suppose Herr Kopf loves Mami, but it makes me angry most of all when she smiles back at him. Doesn't she still love Dawdi? I will try to be glad we have a good shteef-dawdi.

Herr Kopf's daughter Anna Sophia lives with us, too. She's nice and helps with our women's work.

This spring there was something good that happened. The weaver sent George back to us! He has beard hairs, but I still recognized him. Thank the Lord, his health is good. One of Herr Weiser's sons *died* during his apprentice time. Conrad Jr. took that news very hard. Freddie was his favorite brother.

Now it's fall. Adam and Shteef-dawdi came back late yesterday afternoon from working in the woods.

"Governor Hunter says we *still* owe more work. We've been working hard for a long time... *lange zeit!*" Adam complained. "We work more and more and we don't have anything!"

Mami added, "Everybody told us Queen Anne would give us passage and *our own free* land! Didn't she tell Governor Hunter?"

Shteef-dawdi answered, "Ya, but he was supposed to give her naval stuff. Even though they all know the pines here are the wrong kind, Hunter refuses to believe it. He makes us keep trying."

Adam added, "The Queen doesn't like him anymore. Now she's making him use his own money to feed us."

Shteef-dawdi continued, "That's why he just stopped our rations."

Then I understood why George, little Jacob, and I have to gather berries and nuts. Adam shoots little animals like rabbits, and we make stew from deer meat.

Tonight when the six of us sat down for supper at our crude table with benches, Shteef-dawdi told Mami, "Herr Weiser and others went to talk to the Indians."

"To talk about Schoharie?" Mami asked and he nodded.

"How do they know where to find them, the Indians?"

"Mahican Indians here know the ones at Schoharie."

"Are they Mohawks? I heard Frau Zeh talking about them."

He nodded and asked for the bowl of stewed apples.

"Mohawk chiefs told Queen Anne that they'd give her land for us. In return they wanted her to build a fort to protect them. The French attack them, and so do Catholic Indians. They wanted a Protestant chapel, too."

"Why wouldn't the Mohawks attack *us*?" Adam wondered.

"They want peace, like the Indians in Carolina. Remember, we heard about them years ago?"

There were excited voices near our hut yesterday afternoon. We rushed outside to see what was happening. A cold breeze rustled the leaves, all orange, red, and gold. I hoped winter wasn't coming early. Then I saw the men who had just returned from the Indian village. A crowd gathered around them.

"*Guten tag, guten tag!*" Adam greeted Herr Weiser.

"*Wie bischt?*" How are you?

"*Gut, gut.*"

"What did the Indians say?"

"Tell us! Tell us!"

"We talked a long time, with the help of a translator and many hand motions. They spread out grass mats and we shared a pipe of tobacco."

"But can we go?!"

"We have Mohawk permission! We can move! Thanks be to God!"

Herr Weiser warned, "We have much work to do before the snows come. There is no path to our Schoharie land from the Mohawk River. We have to clear a way."

"I'll help!" Herr Braun shouted.

"Me, too!" Adam joined in.

"And me!" Philip Braun added.

I was proud of Adam and Philip.

"Our land is close to a Mohawk planting area, but not very close to their castle."

"Castle?!"

"They have castles?!"

"That's what they call them, but they're not like our castles on the Rhine. It's a cluster of houses made from trees. Each house is long and narrow."

Another man added, "Many families live in each house, a longhouse."

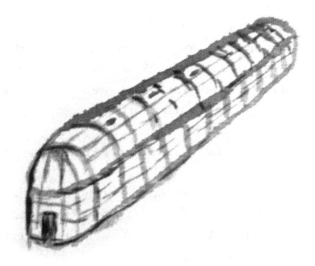

Herr Weiser stressed, "Governor Hunter still says we cannot go. He says the Indians didn't own Schoharie because a man called Bayard bought it a long time ago. But I think Hunter is wrong."

I thought Hunter must be a nasty man. He stopped our rations. Herr Weiser says we can trust the Mohawks. They're nice and will teach us to grow things and make clothes.

But I worried about being with so many Indians, far away from the English, even though no Indians here ever hurt any of us. I hoped Shteef-dawdi will find a way for us to live here instead of going. Some families left here to work on nearby farms. Maybe we could do that.

Last night Shteef-dawdi and Mami were talking softly after we blew out the candle. I listened carefully to every word.

"Many of our friends are going. It will be too hard to survive here. Herr Weiser says that in Schoharie the Mohawks will help feed us and teach us to survive in the wilderness."

"I trust him. He's a good man. I pray he's right," Mami said.

"He says there are settlements at places called Albany and Schenectady where families can stay until the path to our land is ready."

Shteef-dawdi paused then continued, "We should go. It's our dream of our own land, at last!"

"How far would we have to walk?"

"About 75 miles north, up the Hudson to Ft. Orange, some call Albany. Then 15 miles west along the Mohawk River to Schenectady. That's where we'd start walking south to Schoharie, about 25 miles. There's an Indian path the first 5 miles. We have to clear the rest of it."

"That's a *long* way! Can't we stay until the weather gets better in the spring?"

"We have no food. Better to leave soon. People will help us. 'Poor Palatines,' they call us."

I couldn't fall asleep for a long time. I thought about walking so far away through strange woods and rivers. What if there are bad men and bad Indians? And wolves? And witches? We wouldn't have guns. They belong to the English, Mami said.

What if I can't walk that far? Our horses belong to the English, too. What if I can't keep up with the grownups? I hope George could help me care for Jacob, in case he gets tired walking. He's too heavy for me to carry. I'll help take our belongings, dried food, and drop spindle. We'll need it to spin flax and wool fiber. But how will we weave it? We'll need clothes!

Today Adam told us after breakfast what he heard from Conrad.

"The Weiser family is leaving soon to stay at the Schenectady place. But if the weather is too bad they'll stop near Fort Orange at Albany. Dutch people have lived there a hundred years."

"And what's that other place? Skinny-neck?" I asked.

"Schenectady. The Indian Lower Castle is near there. It was a frontier place where the Indians traded with the Dutch."

"Traded? What do Indians have that the Dutch wanted?" Mami asked.

"Beaver furs. They got high prices in Europe. Beaver hats were in style."

"Did Indians want Dutch money?"

"No, metal things like scissors, knives, needles, even kettles."

George had been gathering nuts and came back inside. Suddenly, there was a terrible odor.

"George! Go back outside!" Mami yelled.

"*Raus mit der!*"

"You stink!" Adam exclaimed.

"A skunk got me!"

"*Dumkupp!*"

"Don't you know to stay away from skunks?"

"Go right to the river. Wash yourself! Your clothes, too!"

"Too cold!"

"Take this blanket, but keep it dry!"

He looked at the ground and nodded.

"Here's soap. Don't waste it. We won't have time to make more if we leave here."

Soon after Herr Weiser said the Indians would give us Schoharie land, we packed to travel and began walking up the Hudson. I'm glad the Brauns, Zehs, and Weisers are with us, and there are very many other families.

But not all came. We bid them farewell, *"Macht's gut!"*

Before we left, Mami borrowed scissors from the Brauns and motioned for me to come to her. "Let me cut your hair. It will be easier to keep clean on our trip along the Hudson."

The clippings weren't as blonde as they used to be. I wonder what I look like. I just turned twelve last month.

Adam says we're about halfway along the 75 miles from our hut to Albany. We have to get there before the big snows, and there's not much daylight. The sun comes up late and sets early. We try to walk about five miles every day on the Indian path. Families take turns paddling in two boats somebody borrowed.

Sometimes Adam and Shteef-dawdi carry Jacob. He's only five. George and I help carry things in bundles made from bedding. We're taking household things and dried food like deer meat, sunflower seeds, and nuts.

At first it was very hard for me to walk. My shoes are old and worn. But my legs are getting stronger, and sometimes we sing hymns as we walk to give us energy. We pray for good weather and so far, the snows were light. But my feet get cold whenever we head into cold north wind.

Yesterday evil spirits hurt me while I was using our walking stick to cross a stream. My bundle was tied on my back. I slowly stepped on a rock and put the stick in the stream to balance. The rock was icy and my foot started slipping. I tried to keep from falling, but the drop spindle shifted in my bundle. My foot went in the icy water past my ankle.

"Help!" I screamed. *"Hilfe! Hilfe!"*

Philip and Adam were nearby and turned around.

"Don't move! Keep your other foot dry where it is, on that big flat sunny rock."

I looked down into the stream and saw a trout swim by.

"Give me your hand." Adam reached toward me.

He led me safely across, then built a fire to dry my shoe and stocking while others rested. I was ashamed I held up everyone's travel.

We caught fish from the stream and cooked them over the fire while my things dried. Elk watched us from the woods. It was pretty, with many oaks and birches that had already dropped their leaves. Pines sheltered us from the wind. We thanked God and ate tree nuts.

Then we continued walking until the sun was low. We slept close together for warmth, near a fire to keep wolves away.

January 1713, Schenectady

We rested a few days at Albany, and some families stayed there for the winter. Our family continued walking along the Mohawk River to Schenectady with Herr Weiser's group.

"Weiser is a good leader and knows the Indians," Shteef-dawdi told us.

At Schenectady, some of our men left immediately to clear a twenty-mile path through the woods to our new land, Schoharie. Adam and Shteef-dawdi went with them. They had to make clearing tools because the ones we had before belong to the English. Our men worked so hard and cleared the path in only two weeks!

As soon as they came back, fifty families in our group walked through the snow to the Schoharie wilderness. I'm glad *we're* staying here until spring. The families staying in Albany will go in the spring, too.

Some nice Dutch people here in Schenectady are giving us a home for the winter. Lord bless them! We're so glad to rest and be warm, to wash lice away, and eat good food.

We live with an old couple we call Grossmami and Grosspapi. They like to have us in their house because their own children are big and moved out. Grosspapi enjoys telling stories to Jacob. At first, Grossmami thought Jacob was a girl because his straight blonde hair grew very long on our journey.

Yesterday Grosspapi grinned while he stooped and pretended to be a small child.

"*Kleines Madchen,*" he said to Jacob.

"*Kap,*" he covered his head with his hands.

"*Hut,*" he tried another word for "hat."

"*Rot, rood, red,*" he pointed to Grossmami's red apron.

Jacob nodded, somehow understanding the mixture of Dutch, German, English, and hand movements.

Grosspapi put a basket over his arm.

"*Lopen. Gehen.*" He walked a few steps, bent over to stay small.

"*Woud. Wald.* Woods." He stood like a tree with branches then opened both arms to show many trees.

Jacob eventually caught on that the story was Little Red Riding Hood and giggled with delight when Grosspapi growled like the big bad wolf.

Then George yelled, "Let's play outside in the snow!"

We're happy to have him back with us. We missed him very much when he was sent to live with the weaver.

We laughed and threw snowballs at each other. Our step-sister Sophia played, too. She's almost seventeen, about as old as Adam.

When we rested, Adam said proudly, "Herr Weiser told me that only twenty miles up the Mohawk River is an Indian village called Ticonderoge. Some call it the 'Lower Castle.' It's where Queen Anne just built Fort Hunter."

George wasn't listening.

"Look at that Indian!" he pointed in the distance to an older man with red skin.

"His clothes are English!"

"My dawdi says that's one of the Indian chiefs who went to see Queen Anne. He was baptized a long time ago," Sophia told him.

"Who baptized him?!"

"I don't know," Sophia replied.

"Dutch people. They made the Indians Protestant," Adam liked to impress Sophia.

"Is he the one they call Henry?"

"I think so," Adam continued. "He's part of the Wolf Clan at Ticonderoge."

"Wolf Clan?! What's that?"

"A very big group of Indians. There are three Mohawk clans, Turtle, Bear, and Wolf."

"Do they talk different languages?"

"*Nein*, they talk the same. A picture at a longhouse entrance shows which clan lives there." Adam was showing off what's he'd learned from Herr Weiser.

"How does somebody choose their clan?"

"They *don't* choose. A mother's clan becomes the clan of all her children."

"So boys have to marry their cousins in their clan?"

"Nein, when a boy marries, he leaves his mother's clan and becomes part of his wife's clan."

That seemed strange to me. Men are more important than women. Why didn't the wife become part of her husband's clan?

The Mohawk man we saw in English clothes seemed kindly, but some other Indian men frightened me. They had tattoos and wore deerskin clothes, some embroidered. Their tops with fringes hung over their kilts and leggings. They smoked tobacco pipes. Some had their heads shaven except a strip in the middle that stood up. It was scary, yet funny looking! Adam said those were the warriors.

Today Adam told us, "Last fall, an Indian chief called Quinant was at the meetings about Schoharie with Herr Weiser. The chief invited Weiser's son Conrad to live with his Mohawk family. Herr Weiser said Quinant is trustworthy and it will be good for Conrad to learn Mohawk language. And their ways of living."

To *live* with the Mohawks! He's only seventeen. I'd never do that! He's very brave!

"Did he *order* Conrad to go?!"

"He didn't have to. Conrad agreed because he wanted to get away from his *shteef-mami*."

I tried to imagine Conrad living with all those Indians, and not understanding what anybody said!

When the snow wasn't too deep anymore, we packed to walk to Schoharie. I was sad to leave Grossmami and Grosspapi. I hugged and kissed them good-bye and wished them God's blessing.

"*Auf weidersehn. Gott segen eich.*"

They answered in Dutch and waved as we walked away.

"*Vaarwel!*"

"Mami, may we come back to visit them soon? They're old and might die!"

"Ya, Molly, we'll try, maybe in summer."

I carried our drop spindle and a sack of dried wheat seeds. Shteefdawdi and Adam carried our heavy bundles. George, Sophia, and Mami helped, too, but Jacob was still too small to carry much. It was my job to watch him so he didn't wander off to chase a rabbit or something.

With Herr Weiser as the leader of our big group, we reached Schoharie Creek the second day and walked south along it. We passed new villages started by the fifty families who moved last winter, like Kniskern's Dorf and Garlach's Dorf. They were named after their group leaders. Hartman's Dorf is the biggest. We call ours Weiser's Dorf.

I'm happy that Philip Braun's family, the Zehs, and the Fecks live in our village. I still like when Philip Braun talks to me, and Catharina and Eva Feck are my good friends.

Governor Hunter continues to say that Schoharie doesn't belong to us. The Indians still say he's wrong. They insist they gave it to Queen Anne for us.

By now, five hundred of us Palatines live in Schoharie. Each family has a farm on the flat land near the creek. Our log cabins are small, but bigger than the ones we had when we lived near the Hudson. It's so nice to have our own fertile land.

The big green hills all around protect us. There are strawberries in the fields. The fragrance of honeysuckle is in the breeze. It's pretty, just like when I was very little, at our home across the sea.

Beavers live in the creek where we catch fish. There's a pile of driftwood that we use to walk across the water. I learned that "Schoharie" means driftwood in Mohawk.

A few months ago we planted the wheat and flax seeds we had carried here. It will be more than a year before the flax will be ready to harvest, then much more time until we can prepare the plants for spinning into thread. We'll have to take the thread to a big town many miles away to be woven into cloth because none of us has a loom. How I long for new linen clothing!

But I'm grateful for the deerskin clothes, moccasins, and animal furs the Indians gave us. They also gave us corn to plant and showed us where to find wild potatoes and roots that are safe to eat. When I snuggle under my bearskin on my nice-smelling pine-needle bed, I thank the Lord for the Indians.

Yesterday I asked Mami, "Why are the Indians so kind to us Palatines? They don't like some of the English, nor any of the French people."

"Maybe because Herr Weiser sent young Conrad to live with them. He's still there, you know. Miles away, somewhere around Schenectady, I think."

"But some Mohawks live closer to us. Why isn't he with them?"

"Their closer places are small and not used all year, Herr Weiser says."

Then she agreed, "The Indians are indeed very kind."

I nodded. "Adam told me they taught him and other men how to kill deer without guns. The English have ours."

I continued, "Adam and the men got into a 'V' shape. Then they used rattles to drive the deer into the middle and killed them with bows and arrows."

Mami added, "Adam told me that one day when they were hunting, they heard Frau Zeh screaming. She was hiding behind a tree with her basket of chestnuts and walnuts and crying, 'Panther! Panther!' A Mohawk motioned for the others to stay behind. He and his friends sneaked up on the mountain lion and killed it! We couldn't survive without the Indians!"

Today George and I were fetching water from a spring in pottery jugs.

"George! George! There! Indian girls!" I yelled.

"Where?"

"Toward the noon sun, south, upstream."

"It looks like they're working in their fields."

"Let's go closer."

We walked along the stream, but stayed behind trees so they wouldn't see us. They had long dark braided hair.

"They're your age," George guessed.

"I heard that Indian women and girls tend the crops. Just like our women!"

"I wonder what they think of our small huts. They must see them from the other side of the stream. Even though they're covered with earth and bark."

"Do you think they watch *us*?"

"They might see us at our outdoor bake oven."

"I heard that on the other side of the stream the mountain has a limestone cavern with a hidden waterfall. They could watch from there!"

One day last week I asked, "Mami, when will Adam and Shteef-dawdi be home from Schenectady?"

"Soon. Herr Feck came back yesterday."

"We need our own mill! It's so far for them to go to grind grain. I hope they sold some and bought a big stew kettle for us!"

"And I hope we can buy our own plow horse next year. I don't like to borrow all the time."

"Does Shteef-dawdi know how to build a wagon?"

"Ya, with beech trees. He made a good plow for us, didn't he?"

I nodded.

"When can we get linen cloth? The Indians are kind to give us leather for breeches and jackets. But I wish we had our own cloth."

"I don't know."

I went outside and sat on a rock to daydream about things we might have in our new home, like a sleigh to travel in the snow and musical instruments. I wanted a zither like Dawdi had made for me. Then I cried a little, thinking how much I miss him. I looked back at our sturdy little cabin.

Mami came out. "Come help me make lye. We need more soap."

She gathered white ashes from the fire to turn into lye.

Late that afternoon Adam and Shteef-dawdi returned. They said that Conrad is back home from living with the Indians.

I asked, "When is he coming to see us? We want to hear all about the Indians, don't we George?" He nodded.

"Conrad is very weak. They didn't recognize him when he came back to Weisersdorf. Very skinny, long hair, dressed like an Indian."

"Did he walk all that way?"

"Ya. Good muscles from running and working hard. But he needs food and rest."

Yesterday Conrad came to visit.

"*Velkumm*, Conrad! We haven't seen you for almost a year!"

"Ya, I didn't mind going to the Indians. My dawdi said we need somebody to speak Mohawk."

"Are they kind? The Indians, I mean?" Adam wondered.

"Ya. They like to help people. Chief Quinant is a good man, and I made some good friends. But not all are good."

"Did you meet their chiefs who saw Queen Anne?"

"Ya, King Hendrick was one. I also met a chief called Shikellamy who lives in Pennsylvania in some other tribe, not Mohawk."

"What about the bad ones?"

"They got drunk on homemade beer and strawberry wine, and English rum. Then they'd beat me up. I ran and hid in the bushes. The women would try to stop them."

"Women stop men?!"

"Women are really the rulers. If someone is very bad, he gets banished to the woods. They don't have a jail."

"Do they have a queen?"

"Nein, but clan mothers choose the chiefs. And advise them, too."

"You look too skinny!" I blurted out, even though I knew I should keep quiet.

"Very cold winter. Not much food. Juniper berries kept away hunger feelings."

"Just berries? Didn't you eat other food?!"

"Ya, bread made from corn, beans, nuts, sunflower seeds. And dried things, berries, fish, deer meat. Sometimes fresh rabbit with chestnuts, corn soup, squirrel stew. We ate one meal a day, mid-morning."

"What are their houses like?" Shteef-dawdi asked.

"About a hundred people live in each one. All the women in it are related. When a son gets married, he moves out, to his wife's clan. When a daughter gets married her husband moves in."

That was what we'd already heard when we lived in Schenectady, but Conrad told us more.

"Sometimes they have to make the house bigger."

"How?"

"Build onto the ends. It's made from elm saplings and bark. Very long, narrow, tall." He motioned with his hands and continued.

"An entrance at each end is covered with a large hide. They lift it to enter. Above each entrance is the Wolf Clan emblem. A hole in the top of the house lets out smoke from cooking fires."

"Does rain come in there?" George asked.

"Nein, extra pieces of bark can cover it. They use a long pole to move the pieces. They keep jugs of water nearby to put out fires that might be started by fire-arrows of enemies. But they're at peace now."

He paused and took a deep breath.

"Conrad, would you like some mint tea?" Mami offered.

"*Ya, danke.*"

"Jacob, go pick some mint. You know where, close to the creek."

He got two fistfuls and returned quickly so he wouldn't miss anything.

"Longhouses are always close to a river... on cleared land, so they can see enemies. A high fence, logs standing on end, goes around the group of houses. Women farm inside the fence. They grow corn, squash, and beans altogether on long mounds. Squash grows on the ground, and the beans climb up the cornstalks."

He lifted his arms like high stalks.

"Men fish and hunt. And protect everybody."

Mami poured boiling water on mint and maple syrup and gave a cup to Conrad.

"*Danke.*"

"Did you live in that big house? How did you sleep? Were *all those Indians near you*?!" Jacob's eyes were big with wonder.

He took a sip of tea and answered, "Ya, slept in the longhouse."

"Do they snore?" Adam asked.

"Oh, ya, and have dreams that are very important. I'll tell you about that another time. I'm getting tired now."

Last Sunday afternoon we were sitting on the benches at our table.

"Danke, Frau Kopf," Conrad had finished the cabbage and potatoes Mami made for us. He seemed stronger than the last time we saw him.

Jacob couldn't wait. "*Now* can you tell us how Indians sleep?"

"There's a platform to sleep on, covered with reeds and bearskins. One platform on each side inside the house runs the whole length. That big sleeping platform is divided by hanging mats made of corn husks, woven together. Every family has a sleeping space, open to the center aisle."

"That's not much room!" Mami said.

"What kind of things do they keep in the house?" I asked.

"They store things under the sleeping platform and on a higher one. Clothes, clay pots decorated with zig-zags, knives, bows and arrows. Things they got from the Dutch…guns, brass kettles, metal needles, blankets, cloth. Some things are hung on hooks. Indian women own everything…not men."

He continued, "They believe women should be respected and protected by men."

"Do men dress like you did when you walked home?" Shteef-dawdi asked.

"Ya, tunic, leggings, kilt, deerskin moccasins lined with fur. Snowshoes made from twigs and deer sinew. Some wear a tobacco pouch strapped across their chest. Warriors shave their heads except for a center strip. Some wear feathers on their heads."

"What about girls?" Mami glanced at me and Sophia.

"Long braided hair, fringed cape blouse, skirts, all deerskin. Their skirts stay up because they're folded over a belt. Mothers carry babies on cradleboards on their backs. Little girls play with cornhusk dolls."

"It sounds like they use cornhusks a lot!" I remarked.

"Ya, everybody sits on cornhusk mats. They dry husks by hanging them in bunches over smoking fires. They smoke meat and fish, too."

"Do they start fires like we do when we're in the woods?"

"Ya, special stones, a fire drill, and wood that's charred or rotting. Some fires are made with dried corncobs."

"Conrad! How did you ever survive? You didn't know how to talk to them!" Adam tried to imagine himself living there.

"Pointed to things and they told me names. Hand motions. Facial expressions."

Philip Braun came to our door. My heart raced and I blushed.

"May I listen, too, *bitte*? Conrad told me he was coming here."

"Ya, *velkummen*," Mami answered.

"Mohawk dreams are very important," Conrad continued. "They think supernatural beings send dreams as advice. And that their souls actually experience the dreams. They act them out the next day. Others help."

"That sounds dangerous!"

"During midwinter celebration, they make a game out of guessing each others' dreams."

"Do they play games for fun, like we do?" Adam asked.

"Ya, they think the Creator gave them a game played with a wooden ball, about this big."

Conrad spread his thumb and middle finger to about three inches.

"And wooden sticks that look like big spoons to catch the ball."

"Do girls play, too?" I wondered.

"Only boys and men. Sometimes very many on each team, to settle arguments. Winners are the first to make three goals."

"What else?" George was curious.

"Foot races, like ours. In winter they tell stories around a fire."

Jacob was squirming and bouncing up and down on the bench. It was too much talking for a five-year-old.

"Stop *rutching* around, Jacob."

"May I go play outside?"

Shteef-dawdi nodded.

Mami answered, "Ya, if you find acorns, bring them back. Here's a basket."

Then she turned to Conrad.

"Tell us about Indian food, please."

"Next time I visit. Getting tired."

Conrad left and we talked a while about what we learned. The part about dreaming made me wonder if dreams have a purpose and are sent from God.

I heard a cold wind blow against our cabin.

Philip stayed a little longer to talk to Adam and George. I was happy that he kept glancing at me.

After Philip left Mami told Adam, "Go get Jacob. It's getting too chilly outside."

Shortly, Adam came running in. He was carrying Jacob.

"Snake bite! Hurry! Hurry!"

Shteef-dawdi cut the wound open and sucked out the poison, but it was too late. Mami, Sophia, and I sobbed and sobbed. Adam, George, and Shteef-dawdi were very somber.

There'd been too many deaths already in my life. Why was God doing this?! Was I being punished for sometimes getting angry at Jacob? I loved Jacob! God should know that!

Conrad came back to visit two months later on a rainy day. It was after the harvest, and there wasn't as much farm work.

We sat at our table again and gave thanks for our food...*Dank fur essen.*

"Do you know a few Mohawks live only about a mile from here?" Conrad asked.

"Ya, they help us hunt," Adam said.

"I see women and girls working in their fields," I told him.

"Me, too," Sophia said. She and I like working together on our crops.

George reminded Conrad, "Mami wants to hear more about food."

"Ya, remember I told you that Indian women grow vegetables? Corn, beans, squash, all on the same mound. They harvested pumpkins last month."

"Just like us!" George interrupted.

"They make soup from three kinds of beans. Corn and carrots are in it, too."

Mami said, "The maple syrup they gave us is very good!"

"Ya, they mix it into their corn mush... corn cooked in ashes and washed many times."

"Do they eat apples, berries, and nuts like we do?" Mami wondered.

"Ya, wild potatoes, too. Strawberries are special food. They think their Awehai ancestor held a strawberry plant when she fell from sky. She's their Creator. They make wine from strawberries, too."

Mami continued, "What do they eat in winter?"

"Dried vegetables, fruits, meat, and fish. Mostly kept in baskets and bins in the longhouse. Some kept in pits covered with bark and earth. They dry tobacco, too."

Shteef-dawdi wondered, "I saw men fishing. Where do they get fishhooks?"

"Make them. Bones of small birds. They use spears and nets, too. I guess you know they hunt with arrowheads made from chipped stones?"

Shteef-dawdi answered, "Ya. They hunt elk, deer, moose, bears, beavers, squirrels, turkeys. Even birds like partridges."

"Do men do anything besides hunting? You said women farm and make the important decisions," Shteef-dawdi continued.

"There are special men who have memorized all their laws. They pass them on to young men to memorize."

"Tell us about their warriors, please."

"Long ago they were at war with other Indians. They made peace by dividing into five nations. The Mohawks are one of those Iroquois nations."

"Are they still at peace with other Indians now?" Adam wondered.

"Ya, they believe people should respect all others. And respect everything, including spirits in rocks, trees, streams. They even ask the trees permission to carve a face into them."

"Oh, I wonder what THAT looks like!" I was astounded.

"Very strange."

He continued, "They settle disputes by talking. It's easier now for us to settle disputes with them because I can interpret."

Shteef-dawdi nodded approval.

Conrad continued, "When the two parties agree, they exchange wampum. If no agreement, they drop a wampum belt to the ground."

"What's wampum?"

"Belts of little polished beads. Made from clam shells that came from the place our ship docked down the Hudson. They use it like money."

"Would you show us wampum sometime?" George asked.

"Maybe. There is a Keeper of Wampum. They also use it to record laws, customs, and send messages."

"Did your father get this land for us with wampum?" Adam asked.

"Ya, and traded other things."

Mami asked, "Would you please ask some Indian women to show us how to cure deerskin? Would you translate for us?"

I was surprised he said he would.

"They're generous, share what they know and what they have."

"May I ask Frau Zee and the Fecks, too? Catharina and Eva. The Zeh cabin is big enough for all the women."

"Ya, I'm friendly with an Indian woman named Kahente. Means 'before her time.' And one called Waneek, means 'keeper of the peace.' Her husband is Tawit, means 'nice guy.'"

"What strange names!"

"Names are special. In all the Mohawk Nation, no one else is allowed to have the same name. After the person dies, someone else can use the name. They have no last names."

"I'll try to arrange for them to come. Late one afternoon."

"*Ya, gut, danke!*"

He got up to leave.

"Next time I'll tell you about their ceremonies."

"*Die sunn is am unnergeh.* The sun is setting. Did you bring a torch to keep the wolves away on your walk home?"

"Ya, may I light it in your fire?"

"Ya, *Gott segen eich.* God bless you," Shteef-dawdi replied.

On a bright cold day a few weeks ago, I heard Conrad talking to Adam outside our cabin.

"Two of my Indian brothers are my very good friends and always will be. Someday I will introduce you."

Mami wanted me to set the table before they came inside. We were going to have rabbit stew.

"Molly, *setz der disch.*"

When they came inside we welcomed them by the warm fire.

"Conrad, *guten tag.*"

His fur-lined deerskin moccasins had a little snow on them. He carried his snowshoes, made from hickory branches and deer sinew.

"Guten tag! Frau Kopf, I asked my Indian sister to show you how to cure deerskin for clothing. I will bring her and her daughter soon, before their maple festival."

"*Danke,* Conrad," Mami thanked him and wondered, "Maple festival?"

"Ya, they give thanks to their Great Spirit for the sweet sap. They also have a planting festival, a strawberry festival, corn festival, harvest festival, and a festival to welcome the new year. That one lasts nine days. It starts five nights after the first new moon after the winter solstice."

"Do they sing like we do in church to give thanks?" George asked.

"Mostly chanting and dancing. Counter-clockwise in a big circle for hours and hours. Bare-chested men with tattoos wearing feathers and decorated kilts over leggings. Some have armbands and rattles. They use sticks to beat drums filled with water."

"Where do they get drums?" George asked.

"Make them from hollow logs. Coated with tree resin. Then covered with groundhog skin pulled tight and attached to the bottom."

"You said there's water in them?" Adam asked.

"They fill them through a hole that can be plugged."

"Oh, I'd like to see that!" George interrupted. "Not like church!"

"I think I heard them one day shortly after our new year!" Adam exclaimed and continued, "The wind was strong from upstream, where their small village is."

"That could be. But most festivals are at their large village where I lived, close to Fort Hunter. Or maybe at the downstream village Eskahare. It's across the creek from our most northern village."

"But what I heard wasn't at the right time of year. It was after harvest and before the new year."

"You may have heard them chanting to scare off the Evil Spirit who brings sickness. Then they wear ugly masks."

"Where do they get masks?"

"Make some from corn husks. Or carve them from linden trees. They thank the tree then carve it while a priest chants. Then they cut the tree down, remove the mask, paint it, and put hair on it."

That night I dreamed about Indians wearing ugly masks and dancing around me as I slept. I was so scared I yelled and Mami woke me up.

"Hush, it's only a dream, dear Magdalena. The Indians have always been kind to us, and very helpful. Remember, they showed us where to get wild potatoes and strawberries and how to grow corn. And gave us clothes."

One week later Mami, Sophia, and I walked along the Schoharie Creek to the Zeh's cabin to meet Indian women. Otters played in the water and an elk watched us from the nearby woods. We passed the ford across the creek, formed a long time ago by piles of driftwood. The limestone mountain Onistagrawa on the other side of the creek was still covered with snow. They say there's a hidden waterfall in a cave on that mountain.

Frau Zeh welcomed us inside. Catharina and Eva Feck were already there. Frau Zeh is bigger and stronger than most of our women. Sometimes she talks very loud, too. I'm glad Mami is more like I think a lady should be.

"This is Kahente, and her daughter Waneek," Conrad introduced us.

"*Khwe, khwe,*" they said hello, and we repeated their greeting, as Conrad had told us to do.

Waneek looked as old as Sophia and had long braided hair. She and her mother smiled and gave Mami a wooden bowl as a gift. We knew to say *"nia wen"* as thanks. Then we gave them some metal sewing needles.

They picked up the baskets and deerskin slings they'd carried there. In them were deerskin pieces. The first piece they showed us still had deer hair on it. Then they made a scraping motion a few inches above the skin with a bone knife and showed us a piece with no hair. We nodded our understanding.

They said something to Conrad and he translated, "Remove hair then soak it in water a few days. Then drape it over a log with no bark."

They pulled out a tool from the sling. It looked like a small hoe.

"Use this to scrape flesh, fat, and sinew. Turn it over, remove hair again then wash it."

They showed us a piece ready to be washed. We nodded.

Conrad continue translating, "Twist to dry it, then stretch it with leather thongs on a wooden frame. Then rub with this paste made from deer brain, fat, and water cooked together."

They passed around a little earthenware container of the stuff to let us feel it. I just looked at it. It seemed so unpleasant, but I smiled to them. Eva and Catherine Feck didn't touch it either. Frau Zeh stuck her fingers in it.

Waneek said something to Conrad, and he continued, "Soak it again in water, twist dry, and rub paste again. Then put it on a tripod by a fire to smoke it."

They proudly displayed a finished product.

I said, *"Nia wen."*

I hoped I would see Waneek again. I wanted to know how she got her name and what she does to help her mother.

"Do you live in a village close to us?" I looked at Conrad and asked him to translate my question.

"Hen," she answered.

Conrad said, "Ya," then added, "I met them when they traveled to visit the Lower Castle where I lived."

Frau Zeh gave everyone mint tea before we said farewell, *"O nen."*

I was sitting by the Schoharie Creek with Tillie, my pet turtle, late on Sunday afternoon. The sky was beautiful blue, the trees pretty colors. I saw little Jacob's grave and said a prayer for his soul. The acorn I planted when he was buried is just starting to sprout. It will be a fine, strong oak.

We've been in our Schoharie home over a year now. I'm happy again, like I was when I was eight, before the bad winter when we left the Palatine. I'll be fourteen this month, still skinny as ever, but as tall as Mami and still growing.

I have friends in Weisersdorf, but I don't know anyone in the other *dorfs*. Mami says there are about 500 of us Palatines! Each *dorf* has many farms, but none has a church building, a store, or a gristmill. The grownups take our wheat all the way to Schenectady to grind. They buy supplies there, too. We made sleighs to carry things in winter.

I saw Sophia walking toward me along the creek. She's very pretty, with long blonde hair. I like her very much.

"Molly, is that your special turtle?"

"Ya, want to hold her? Her name is Tillie, for Matilda."

I handed her to Sophia. As she petted her shell, she said, "Mami wants me to pull up some flax plants tomorrow. Will you help?"

I nodded. Soon after we came to Schoharie, we planted a half acre of flax, but we'll need at least another full acre to make enough cloth for the six of us. Tomorrow we'll pull some green flax and let it dry a few days in the sun. When it turns into brown straw we'll bundle it and bring it in. Next spring we'll put it back out on the grass in the mornings and let the dew dissolve the stuff that holds it to the woody stalk. Then we'll beat it to take out the seeds, plant some seeds, and sell some.

"I carried our drop spindle all the way from home across the sea. It will be nice to use it again to spin flax thread," I said.

Sophia reminded me, "It will still be quite a while. After we take out the seeds, we have to crush it, separate the fibers from it, and pull it through the hackle."

"What's that?"

"It looks like a brush with metal bristles. I wonder if we have one?"

"I don't think so. Maybe we can borrow one from the Fecks."

"Adam will have to hang the fibers very high so the mice don't get them."

I remembered Mami's old mami, *Grossmami*, spinning when I was very little. A warm feeling came over me. She was so kind and loving.

I used to watch her and Mami make soap, too. They boiled rainwater and ashes in a big kettle over the fire until all the ashes went to the bottom. Then in went some lard from a cooking pan and a little oatmeal. Mami stirred it a long time then put it in greased wooden molds and covered it with wet cloths.

"Molly, Molly, are you daydreaming?" Sophia's voice interrupted my thoughts.

"Oh! Yes, I guess so. I was thinking that someday my children will watch me make soap and spin thread here in Schoharie."

"*Dunner Vetter!*" Shteef-dawdi was very angry.

"Must you curse, Jacob?!"

Mami never swears and doesn't like anyone else swearing.

"They want us to *pay* for our land here. It's already *ours*! We don't owe money! When Herr Weiser met with the Indians, they said they gave it to Queen Anne for us."

"Who wants money now?"

"Seven Englishmen. *And* a Dutch man named Vrooman."

"Didn't Governor Hunter tell them its ours?"

"You know Hunter has never been kind to us. We don't have Queen Anne to protect us anymore. She died in August, remember?"

"What about her husband, the king? He's German, isn't he? He should care about us. This land belongs to him now."

"Doesn't matter. They say King George acts just like one of those princes we fled years ago. Rich, uncaring about peasants."

"Who *are* these men who want money?"

I became upset as I listened to their talking. I fought back the tears in my eyes. We've made such a nice home here. We have no money to pay to keep it.

"Hunter is giving a patent for our land to men called Seven Partners. They're rich friends of his. They asked for the land last spring."

"Oh, no! What about the Dutch man?"

"Vrooman said he bought 340 acres of this land from some Indians earlier this year. Conrad says some Indians think the Creator gave all land to everybody. When they get drunk, they'll sign any agreement without knowing what it means. Maybe some of them did sign something for Vrooman."

Just when I was happy again, people were threatening us. Why does God let them do bad things?

"What can we *do*?!" Mami's voice quivered.

"Our ancestors were stubborn, and so are we! We're *shtorrkeppich*! We'll fight again!"

Shteef-dawdi came running back to our cabin. He yelled, "Herr Weiser is going to be arrested! Hunter is after him, called him a ringleader."

Adam looked up from the pile of wood he was chopping.

"Ringleader?!"

"The English know we tore down Vrooman's cabin and let our cattle trample his crops. They're saying it's Weiser's fault. A sheriff is coming for him!"

"But Weiser is no more at fault than all of us. We all agree Vrooman was on *our* land. I don't understand why the English are calling *us* squatters. We worked so hard to turn this into good farms!"

I looked across the creek at the large mountain Onistagrawa. Adam had told me Vrooman also claimed much of the land there.

Shteef-dawdi added, "The Indians are still our friends. They agree that Vrooman doesn't own this land, even though the English tried to get them on their side with money and rum."

I silently prayed to God for strength and guidance. I was scared there would be fighting. I didn't want Shteef-dawdi and Adam and George to be in danger. And Conrad and Philip and all the other men. We don't have as many men and guns as the English. What are we to do?

Magdalena Zeh had a meeting at her cabin and told everybody her idea.

"We women have to be the ones who punish the sheriff when he comes to collect money and arrest Herr Weiser. We won't be punished as severely as men."

"How can we do that?" Frau Feck wondered.

"If there are enough of us, one man won't stand a chance. We have to be fearless and strong."

Frau Zeh is a large woman with good muscles from working on the farm.

She said, "All you women, talk to your husbands. Tell me if you'll be in our group to meet the sheriff when he comes. We'll take him by surprise. I'll get women from our other villages, too, for our mob."

The following week we had word that Sheriff Adams was on his way on horseback. Magdalena Zeh had prepared the women for his arrival.

"We'll go north to the bridge to meet him by surprise after nightfall. First we have to drag him off his horse," she'd explained to them.

Mami went with the group, but Sophia and I were forbidden to go. We were greatly relieved when Mami returned safely later that night.

"What happened?! Tell us, tell us!"

Our whole family talked at once.

"Frau Schmidt walked into the path when we heard his horse coming. He slowed to avoid hitting her. Then we all came out of the woods. We knocked him off his horse."

"Didn't he fight back? Did he use his gun?"

"We took his gun away from him. We all kept punching him and tied his hands behind his back."

"Then what? Where is he?"

"Frau Zeh ripped a loose board from the bridge and beat him, badly. Probably broke a rib and damaged one of his eyes."

"Oh my, that woman is heartless," Sophia said.

"Then she showed us how to tie him up completely and string him up to his horse. But it gets worse!"

We looked at one another, wondering what more Mami could tell us!

"Frau Zeh stood over him, lifted her skirts, and doused him with her urine! Then she sent him on his way, dragged on the ground by his horse."

It's been almost two years since Governor Hunter started trying to make us pay for this land. Shteef-dawdi went to Albany in the fall of 1715 and officially became an English citizen. Everyone thought it might help make Hunter treat us better if our men became citizens, but it hasn't changed anything.

Many families are talking about moving away! I don't think I could bear moving again!

Mami noticed me thinking. I was worrying, wondering where would we go if we got thrown off our land.

She said, "Molly, you're so deep in thought. Get busy! We have to make our fields ready to plant."

"Mami, what will we do if Governor Hunter makes us leave?"

"I don't know, dear. The men will work something out. Herr Weiser is talking about going to London to appeal to King George."

"Would he take Conrad with him?"

"I don't know. But I haven't heard anyone say that."

"Could the king make Hunter let us stay?"

"He could, but they say he doesn't like us. He thinks we're disloyal peasants who left the German princes. He's German, remember."

"What does Herr Weiser think he could do in London?"

"There's something called a Board of Trade there. They might listen to our story."

Sophia came to help us in the fields. I think she and Adam are going to marry. I heard Shteef-dawdi and Mami talking about that being a good match. And Philip and Sophia seem to love one another.

I wonder who will be chosen for me to marry in a few years. I hope it's Philip Braun, but he might marry one of the Feck girls. Their families are good friends. There aren't any other boys I like as much as Philip, except Conrad, but he has his eye on Anna Eva Feck, and she on him.

Conrad unexpectedly walked up from the creek.

"Guten Tag, Frau Kopf!"

He nodded at the three of us.

"I came to tell Herr Kopf about a meeting. Governor Hunter wants to meet with three men from each village to talk about our land. My father would like your husband to be one of the men from Weisersdorf."

"He's over that way, with Adam and George," she pointed.

"Is it good news for us?" Sophia asked.

"Nein, I'm sorry to say. Hunter wants us all to agree to pay for the land, or else move away."

My stomach became upset and I felt like crying. I knew we couldn't pay.

He continued, "But my father won't give up. He's arranging passage from Philadelphia to London. He wanted to leave from New York, but Hunter won't let him."

A few years ago, Hunter met with men from every village, but our families could not agree what to do. Some wanted to stay and try to pay for the land. Many wanted to leave.

Some already have gone all the way back down the Hudson to where we lived before. Some crossed the Hudson into New Jersey. Others went west from here.

We stayed and waited for good news from Herr Weiser in London. Then, after not having heard from him for a long time, we learned of his very bad trip. His ship had been robbed by pirates. He had no money when he landed in London and had been put into debtors' prison!

Conrad said that after he was released, he told the Board of Trade our story. He told how Hunter abandoned us when the English idea of making naval stuff from pines didn't work. But the board sided with Hunter! What are we to do?!

Adam just told Shteef-dawdi, "Conrad has been talking to the Indians about places to move. Now that he and Anna Eve are married, they'll be starting a family soon. Sophia and I would like to leave, too. Will you come?"

Shteef-dawdi was cautious. "Maybe. We have to know the details. Might be as bad, or worse."

His brow was furrowed and the sun gleamed from the top of his head that used to be covered with dark brown hair.

Conrad continued. "One place is in Pennsylvania. The Indians there aren't Mohawks, but some are friendly with Mohawks I know. Those other Indians might help us."

"Would we have to buy land from them?"

"I don't know yet. Maybe William Penn already bought land from them when he welcomed all people, all religions."

My fears were becoming reality. I dreaded leaving our home yet again! We made this ours!

Our crops are doing well, and we have animals now. We even have enough flax for me to use my drop spindle each winter to make thread. We have it woven in Schenectady into linen cloth.

I like the people in our village and have Indian friends. I still dream about marrying Philip and having our very own family farm here, but that may never happen.

Adam's voice interrupted my thoughts.

He was telling Shteef-dawdi, "We're going to send a few men from Weisersdorf to explore a route to Pennsylvania land. Much of the trip would be on the Susquehanna River. Indian guides agreed to go with them," he seemed hopeful. "But there's much wilderness along the way."

Pennsylvania! I heard people talk about Germans who live there, near Philadelphia. Maybe it would be good to live there.

I have wonderful news! Shteef-dawdi and Herr Braun decided that Philip and I should marry soon! Thinking about that makes me very happy. I do love him very much.

Last week the men reported about their exploring trek to a branch of the Susquehanna River.

"It's going to be a *very* difficult journey," they warned.

I recognized most of them from church services in Weisersdorf. Mami said a few were from Hartmansdorf. None from the other villages. They all looked so strong, with big muscles.

The elder Herr Rieth began, "Thank all who helped cut a narrow trail from Schoharie Creek through the woods to Susquehanna headwaters. We'll have to make that trail wider for pack animals. We'll use them to carry household things, tools, clothes, seeds, guns."

"It's a very difficult climb over that mountain just west of here," someone added.

"Ya, after we leave Schoharie Creek and go west along Panther Creek, there's a very steep climb up to Summit Lake."

"Is that where all creeks on its west side flow to the Susquehanna, but on the east side, to the Delaware River?"

"Ya, that's so."

"We were able to find the headwaters of Charlotte Creek on the other side of Summit Lake. Farther on, where Charlotte Creek flows into the Susquehanna, we'll camp and make canoes."

"Some of us who are staying here will help the group get to Charlotte Creek headwaters."

"That's very kind. Very much welcomed."

I remembered how hard it was to walk along the Hudson. And how much I hated sleeping in the wilderness. May the Lord grant me the strength and courage to do this! We probably wouldn't go with the first group, but maybe later.

My dream of a homestead here with Philip has been shattered. He noticed my despair and reached to hold my hand.

"Most will make canoes and rafts to float down the Susquehanna. But a few young men will have to go a different route, over land and along part of the Delaware River with our cattle. We can't put cattle in canoes, can we?!"

He chuckled and continued, "And the banks of the Susquehanna are too steep and craggy to drive cattle along that part of our route. The young men and cattle will arrive at Tulpehocken later, after the canoe group."

Somebody asked, "Tul-pe-what?"

"Tulpehocken, 'land of the turtles' in Indian language. Our new land."

Herr Rieth's brother continued, "We'll be on the big river for about 400 miles. If conditions are good, we can go 30 miles a day."

"How will you know when to leave the river?"

"We would stop for guidance at a Delaware Indian village called Shamokin on the Susquehanna. Its chief, Shikelemy, is a friend of the Mohawks and the Weisers. They met him at the first talks about Schoharie land."

"Would you leave the Susquehanna there?"

"No, farther south, at the mouth of a creek called 'Swatara.' There's a white man's cabin there, on the east side of the Susquehanna. John Harris lives there."

"And then what?!"

"Up the Swatara, then a short trek over a gravel ridge to the headwaters of another creek, called 'Tulpehocken,' our creek."

"My family will be ready to go with the first group very early next spring." Herr Walborn already had his mind made up.

He continued, "We have to reach the new land early April. Prepare it for spring planting. Otherwise, we won't have food for next winter."

"My family will go with you," another agreed. He had no very young children.

"Who else?"

"We'll go if it's true that Pennsylvania's governor came to Albany to tell us we have his permission to settle there."

"Yes, it's true. Governor William Keith came to meet with us. Our land is on the frontier between the Europeans and the Delaware Indians."

"Oh, no! Will the Indians attack us?"

"They're friendly now. At first they weren't, the governor said. But later their chief Sassoonan agreed to move. They went a little farther west to give us the Tulpehocken land. I don't know what they got in return."

"Is the land close to the Philadelphia Germans?"

"Nein, seventy miles west."

"Good for farming?"

"We'll have to clear it, but they said it's good farmland."

"We have to learn quickly how to build canoes!"

"Conrad will teach us every afternoon down by the creek, starting tomorrow."

"Mami, may I go and learn, too?" I asked and she nodded.

Fifteen families have already said they're going to leave early spring, including the Rieth families. Conrad said he and Anna Eve and their family will go later.

Shteef-dawdi told us maybe we'd go with the second group, after we had word that everything was good there. Adam and Sophia want to come with us, even though they have an infant daughter. But my brother George and his new wife Anna Christina Elizabeth Walborn don't want to travel until their infant is older. Philip said his family would go when we do.

The next day Philip and I went to learn to build canoes. Conrad was a good teacher. It was an unusually pleasant late fall day, graced with birdsong and a clear blue sky.

Conrad reviewed tree names as he pointed to each, "… oak, walnut, birch, beech, ironwood, chestnut, hickory. The Mohawks taught me to thank a tree before taking its life. Everything has a soul."

"Our Indian guide had pointed to elms, chestnuts, hickory for canoes," one of the men who had been in the exploratory group noted.

"Yes, a sturdy, tall white elm with no branches on the lower trunk. You can peel its bark lengthwise in large sheets. Then lay it flat on the ground with stones. Let's find one. Chestnut will work, too."

We all met afternoons until we had made a canoe. Philip worked with them. I helped. One day the men made ribs and sideways supports from a hickory tree.

I tried to imagine sitting in a canoe on a very large river like the Rhine. I knew how to swim, but I was fearful. And what of the small children, like Sophia had?!

Then I remembered one of the Feck girls had wished me a happy birthday last month, the day *before* my birthday. That's a bad omen. I worry bad luck will come to me on our trip down the river. Will I die in the water?

"Goodbye, my dear friend," Mami hugged Frau Walborn as her family embarked with the first group to go to Tulpehocken.

She replied, "May the Lord bless and keep you and your family safe. We will see you next year."

They tried to carry as many of their household goods as would fit on a small wagon. The Walborn children carried a few things in sacks on their backs.

Adam, Shteef-dawdi, and Philip are going with them over land, to help them reach the river and make canoes. Then they'll return to us.

Philip and I have recently been married. I'm overjoyed! He's my true love. But I doubt we'll ever have our own family and farm in Schoharie, like I've dreamed.

We live with Mami and Shteef-dawdi now. Adam and Sophia have their own cabin, and George and Elizabeth have their own, too. The young Weiser couple, Conrad and Eva, had a baby son last year and asked Philip and me to be his baptismal sponsors.

They say there will be enough land there for each family to have a nice little farm on the Tulpehocken Creek, close to the place the Mill Creek flows into it. There are beautiful mountains nearby. I imagine our own little place. But it's going to be hard work to start all over yet again!

Last summer, there was word from the Mohawks that the Algonquin Conoy Tribe scout Thomas, had seen our people near the Swatara. He had reported it to the English in the spring. Months later we heard that they were well and are working the land. The Lord has protected them!

We're making final preparations to go soon. Philip and I will join Shteef-dawdi, Mami, Adam, Sophia, and other families. Mami and I will help Sophia with her small children, Jacob and Susannah. George and Christina are expecting their second baby soon and will stay in Schoharie until later. Their son Jacob was one year old last November.

Shteef-dawdi will take our horse to carry dried food, seeds, clothing, guns, and other things like farm tools, and of course, my drop spindle.

"Why did you *do* that?!" Philip was upset with me.

"I thought it would get us free of the rocks. I'm sorry! I'm so sorry!"

I wiped tears from my cheeks.

We were near the shore in our canoe, but drifting downstream. *Backwards!*

Philip held his paddle in the water and was trying desperately to turn our canoe around. I remembered that I had been wished a happy birthday before my real birthday last year and was sure that brought on this bad luck. I feared we might be badly hurt by crashing into rocks.

Shteef-dawdi was shouting instructions to Philip.

"Tell Molly to put her paddle in the water. That side," he pointed.

"Just hold it there, in the water, don't move it."

"Ya," we both answered.

"Now Philip, you paddle gently like this," he motioned.

We began turning! I was relieved.

I felt so guilty. It was my fault we'd turned backwards. We had drifted too close to shore, I thought. So I reached out with my paddle and shoved hard. Too hard, and not balanced by a shove from the other end of our boat.

It could have been a disaster! We could have crashed hard into rocks. We could have lost everything we were carrying. I was so upset I was shaking.

"It will be all right," Philip said in a calm voice. "I'm sorry I spoke with anger."

He's such a dear sweet husband and I want to please him.

We had left Schoharie the end of March. Back then, we loaded what we could on our workhorse and carried the rest in sacks. The walk up to Summit Lake was very difficult. The ground was muddy and slippery. Some children, too young to walk, had to be carried. I tried to help Sophia and Adam carry their little Jacob, but I wasn't strong enough to carry him far.

When we reached the great Susquehanna I helped make our canoe. Conrad had taught us well. I remembered to thank the trees before we cut them down. I hope they understood German.

This is our third day on the river. The water hasn't been rough, but icy cold. I can't sleep at night because the ground is so frigid and the wind blows hard. Wild animal sounds wake me when I do fall asleep.

We're trying to go 30 miles each day on the water. On this part of the river, our farm animals are being driven on a path that follows the river, but soon some of our single men will head east and take the cattle on a different, slower route. We won't have any of the things they're carrying when we arrive. But how blessed we are that those who settled there last year will help us.

My dream of our very own farm and family has come true! We were welcomed a few years ago by the first families who arrived here. More have come each year, but Conrad Weiser and Eva are waiting until next year to bring their family. The Zeh family came this spring.

The Rieth families were among the first to build their homes, plant gardens, and sow grain. Lennert, Niclaus, Fredrick, and George Rieth are all here. They had already started Lutheran church services and began building a stone springhouse and gristmill before we arrived. Last year they built a church building. We call it Rieth's Church.

As soon as we arrived, we planted our own crops. Philip and I and our infant Philip Junior live next to Adam and Sophia along the Tulpehocken Creek. Mami and Shteef-dawdi live on the other side of Adam. We're all very close to the church.

Yesterday my dear husband surprised me when he said, "Molly, I may have some time this winter to build a zither."

"Oh, Philip, that would be wonderful!"

I gave him a hug and replied, "I could strum while I sing hymns to our baby in the cradle you made."

"There's a fine black cherry tree we cut when we cleared our land. Good wood for the zither. I can use glue the Indians taught us to make from deer hoofs, and make strings from animal gut."

What a fine Christmas we will have with our baby, here on our own farm. I thanked God for blessing us after twenty years of turmoil.

We'll have sauerkraut for good luck on New Years Day. I'll start fermenting it soon after the harvest.

Then I sang a hymn.

"Fairest Lord Jesus, Ruler of all nature, O Thou of God and man the Son, Thee will I cherish, Thee will I honor, Thou, my soul's glory, joy and crown... Fair are the meadows, fairer still the woodlands, Robed in the blooming garb of spring; ...Fair is the sunshine, Fairer still the moonlight, And all the twinkling starry host...."

We'd finally found our heaven on earth.

AFTERWORD

Having survived decades of hardship together, the Tulpehocken families remained a close-knit group with many intermarriages. Baptisms, marriages, and burials were recorded at Rieth's Church (Reeds Church) and survive to this day. My own paternal ancestors include the Loesch, Braun, Schaeffer, and Rieth families.

Magdalena Loesch, who died in Tulpehocken in 1769, was my seventh great-grandmother. In 1728 she and Philip had their first child, Philip Jr. Thirty years later, Philip Junior's daughter Anna Maria was born. She married Peter Rieth, and their son Christian had a daughter Margaret. Margaret's daughter Kate was my great-great-grandmother.

Printed in the United States
By Bookmasters